TITLE

THE HORRIBLE DAUNT

BY Sidra Mohsin

CHAPTER 1:
Booking Fate

He headed to the real estate agent's office, returning home from college, left his vehicle in the third vacant parcel and strolled delicately there. He pushed open the entryway and made proper acquaintance! I'm Aiden Donald'. 'Ideal to meet you Sir! Plunk down. I'm Harold' welcomed the real estate agent delicately. Aiden plunked down on the delicate cowhide seat and warmly greeted Harold. 'I'm here looking for an Apartment for lease' clarified Aiden, 'What Type?' asked the real estate agent. 'Fundamentally, Me and my companion (Matt) need a condo, one that is close to the Garamond University. Our old Apartment was all in all too a long way from it,' said Aiden. Harold took out a record from the second Drawer in his sparkly wooden table and looked through it. He took out one of the papers in the document and showed it to Aiden. Aiden held that paper. It was appended for certain Pictures of a condo. Aiden read the data cautiously. It read:

Spic and span third Floor Apartment for lease in Brown Sea Apts! All around outfitted. 2 Blocks from the Famous Garamond University! 1 Bedroom, 1 Bathroom, 1 Stylish Eat-in Kitchen, Spacious Closet, Shiny Wooden floors. Ideal for a family or a Group of companions! This Apartment building was worked in 1938!

Subsequent to perusing the subtleties of this loft, Aiden cherished it! 'It's totally awesome, and It meets every one of the necessities' said he. 'You can visit this

Apartment for a request on Monday' Harold said. Aiden mulled over everything and afterward concurred that he would stay with this loft on Monday with Matt. 'Alright, Sir! Kindly advise prior to showing up at Brown Sea Apts' said the real estate professional. Aiden gave the thumbs up and left the workplace. He strolled over to his vehicle, sat inside and drove back to his old loft. He went to his loft, opened the entryway and saw that Matt was at that point hanging tight for him on the table. 'I have discovered an Apartment! It's only 2 Blocks from our college' said Aiden in bliss. 'Truly!? What's the Apartment building name?' asked Matt in dismay. 'Earthy colored Sea Apts... ' answered Aiden. 'Goodness! Alright, I am beginning to pack my stuff, you can pack yours' Matt said. The two of them went to their rooms and began pressing their stuff. Aiden pressed his garments and Other things in his Big Blue bag. He kept his gathered bag in the TV relax and went into the kitchen to make some espresso for himself. He drank the espresso and

Started cleaning the condo. He then, at that point, called the Landlord of their present condo. 'Hello! Mr. Earl. Me and Matt are leaving this condo, as this one was a long way from our college, so we have tracked down another' said Aiden apprehensive, as Mr. Earl was a touchy man. 'At the point when will you leave?' asked Mr. Earl in a surly way. 'We'll go to visit the loft on Monday (Tomorrow) and afterward we'll move in that condo on Tuesday or Wednesday' clarified Aiden. 'Alright! Advise me on the day when you'll leave, so I'll come and take this current Apartment's keys' Confirmed Mr. Earl. Aiden finished the call with an 'alright!'. He went to Matt's space to inquire as to whether he had pressed his stuff and tidied up the room. Matt was flashing up his bag. 'I'm resting, it's 10:03 pm. We'll need to get up early tomorrow, You ought to rest too' said Aiden in a languid voice. Aiden went to his room after he took a container of cold water from the cooler, kept it on his bedside table and rested. Aiden experienced rest loss of motion all the time, however not regular, that is the reason he generally kept virus water adjacent to him, so at whatever point he came into his faculties subsequent to experiencing rest loss of motion, he would drink cold water which would quiet him down. At 12:45 am, Aiden's eyes opened to see seeing a tall lady remaining toward the side of the room, he had never seen this lady. She was wearing a battered white dress, she was highlighting the left and was mumbling something unintelligible. He attempted to move his arms and legs, obviously, they wouldn't move. The lady came nearer and said that was presently obviously discernible 'Don't go to the spot, it's the place where me and my family ... ' Then, she disappeared like a phantom. Aiden was as yet engrossed with his contemplations, pondering what the lady had said and what place she was looking at, during this, he didn't understand that his rest loss of motion had finished. He went to one side and ultimately nodded off. He woke up toward the beginning of the day at 9:04 am,brushed his teeth, changed garments and went to the kitchen to make some espresso. Matt didn't awaken yet, so Aiden drank his espresso and went to the close by park for a run. He and Matt took later classes at college, so Aiden had concluded that first he would go to visit the Brown Sea Apts and afterward, he would go to his college. While he was running, he saw a dull outline of somebody in his fringe vision. He looked behind, yet it was nothing. He kept on running for 1 hour and got back at 10:30 am. He cleaned up, changed garments and afterward went to his low maintenance work. He worked at an eatery as a lesser gourmet expert for 4 hours per day. Today, when he arrived at the eatery, there were a ton of orders for a Hawaiian pizza, so every one of the culinary experts cooperated to make so many Hawaiian pizzas. Aiden was anxious with practically everything, except he needed to do this work, assuming he needed to bear the cost of additional instruction. He labored for 4 entire hours and afterward returned home at 3:00 pm in the early evening. At the point when he got back home, Matt was at that point there, he had gotten done with his low maintenance task ½ an hour prior Aiden. They had lunch and afterward called the real estate professional. 'We are staying with the loft quickly,' said Matt. 'Alright! Sir, Thanks for illuminating' answered Harold.

Chapter 2:

Beginning of Horror

Both the companions sat in the vehicle. Aiden was beginning the vehicle, when he discovered that he had neglected to top off the vehicle with fuel the previous evening. They escaped the vehicle and took a taxi. Aiden and Matt both sat in the rearward sitting arrangement, coming, the driver began discussing arbitrary things generally identified with legislative issues. 'I don't have the foggiest idea why this president couldn't care less with regards to his kin and he's continually looking at further developing innovation in the country. Innovation is the thing that destroyed this world. If not intended for this innovation, individuals would've been nearer to one another,' said the driver. Matt feigned exacerbation overlooking the driver's discussion to himself. After around 22 minutes, they arrived at the apartment complex. The driver asked, highlighting the structure 'is this your drop-off place?' 'That's right! That is our objective. We'll leave, Thank you for the ride' said Matt while distributing the cash to the cab driver. The driver yelled 'Stop! Stand by... This structure, it's ccc cc..' 'Ccc, what?' asked Aiden with an apparently irritated face. 'This structure is ccc... Old! No doubt! This structure is truly old' said the driver and drove off as quick as possible. Matt and Aiden checked out one another with a befuddled look. 'Presumably, he was going to say that this structure is Capacious' said Aiden. 'Definitely! You're correct' said Matt and disregarded it. They were so bustling agonizing over the subject, that they scarcely saw Harold sitting tight for them in the entryway of Brown Sea Apts. Harold called out 'Hello! Both of you, Come in here. The meeting time will be over soon' 'Coming! Sorry for being late,' said Aiden and the two of them hurried in the anteroom. They shook hands and stepped in the lift. The lift was tasteful and perfect, contrasted with the old and corroded structure. Aiden and Matt preferred the structure up till now. They at long last arrived at the third floor, Both the companions followed Harold to an old loft. It's entryway was truly old, aside from that every one of them could feel a substantial air around that condo. Harold took out a couple of keys from his pocket, embedded one of them in the keyhole and opened the entryway. While Harold was keeping the keys in his pocket, Aiden pushed ahead to turn the door handle and enter the loft. Right now, he saw some red fluid on the door handle. He went ballistic and told it to Harald. Harald immediately pushed him back, took out a hanky from his pocket and cleaned the stain. 'Ruined children wander this structure around evening time, seeing this loft vacant, they paint this present condo's entryway or door handle, yet relax, it will not occur now' said Herald certainly. Aiden gestured and entered the condo, Matt could feel that there was an off thing. He murmured to Aiden 'Do you feel it?' 'What?' asked Aiden. 'The creepy climate!' answered Matt. 'Gracious! Please! It was locked for a ton of time, that is the reason it seems like that' answered Aiden. Matt actually accepted that something was not typical here. The two of them went into the room. Aiden saw a little shape drawn with pencil on the divider, He bowed down to take a gander at it cautiously. It was a Pentagram, he went nuts, he called Matt to check out it and, indeed he was frightened as well. They went to Harold who was in the kitchen actually looking at the water from the tap. 'What's the historical backdrop of this house?' asked Matt. 'It hasn't got a lot of history, only 2 families have lived here before you. The first left, since they moved to the adjoining city and nobody realizes what befell the second one, So might you want to take this loft? It's lease is sensible and all things considered, it's close to your college,' remarked Harold. Aiden eased off by how demanding the real estate agent was, however Matt idea in the event that it has no set of experiences, it very well may be a decent condo. Both Matt and Aiden escaped the condo, Harold locked it again and took Matt and Aiden in his vehicle to his office for consenting to the arrangement papers and different installments or marks. Matt marked the papers, on the grounds that Aiden wasn't feeling right, he was feeling queasiness. After some time, the condo's property manager showed up at the workplace. She was a fat elderly person named Ms. Analise with light hair, badly crumpled face and wore a scarf. She welcomed her forthcoming inhabitants with joy. 'Much obliged for living in this loft, after a long time it got opened' said Ms. Analise. 'Indeed, we were looking for a decent loft close to our college lastly, we discovered an enthusiastic condo,' answered Matt. 'Goodness! Definitely, This spot is loaded with life and past-recollections' proceeded with Ms. Analise. 'What recollections?' asked Aiden. The real estate agent gave a sidelong look to the old woman and she said 'No... Nothing! Simply some great recollections of past occupants' ,She proceeded 'Farewell! I'll need to go now, you young men can take the Apartment keys from Harold' and Ms. Analise surged out of the workplace, gotten her vehicle and drove going. Aiden and Matt, somewhat went nuts, took the keys from Harold, paid him his bonus and said 'alright! Thus, I have given you additional cash, when Ms. Analise would go to your office tomorrow, offer this to her as a development lease'.

Harold gestured while keeping the cash in the cabinet. Both the companions headed to their old condo, they had effectively employed a truck, so they put all their stuff and required things in the truck and went to their new loft. They opened the loft and stepped in there for the subsequent time, yet they could in any case feel the weighty climate. 'Wouldn't you say, we moved here excessively quick without thinking, I mean, we just visited it today' said Matt. 'Good gracious! No!' said Aiden. 'What?!' asked Matt in shock by the abrupt change in Aiden's demeanor. 'We needed to go to the college, there is still time, we'll set the stuff up around evening time or tomorrow, Come on! How about we go to the college,' said Aiden while getting the vehicle keys. They got back from college at 10:00pm. They just ate a microwave sandwich for supper, as they weren't excessively partial to food. Aiden was changing sides while resting ceaselessly, yet couldn't nod off. He went to one side, when he saw a lady, a similar lady he saw previously. Aiden figured he may be experiencing rest loss of motion once more, yet he wasn't right, this time the lady was genuine! Aiden yelled and afterward, he dropped. Matt got up and approached Aiden's room. He thumped on his entryway, yet saw that his entryway was locked. Matt called 911 in a crisis, as he was freezing. The shout that he heard was truly noisy and obviously showed that Aiden was in torment. The Ambulance showed up in a little while, Aiden was taken to the specialist. 'What befell him?' asked Aiden to Dr. Oliver. 'He may have had a terrible dream. Does he take sadness pills?' asked Dr. Oliver. 'I haven't seen him taking any pills, all I know is that he experiences rest loss of motion much of the time' answered Matt. 'Well! I imagine that this kind of circumstance for the most part occurs if an individual is presented to another climate. Did he visit another spot today?' asked Dr. Oliver. 'Indeed! We moved into another condo today' addressed Matt. 'Relax! He will be fine soon, he simply needs some rest' said the Doctor finishing the discussion. Matt headed toward the room where Aiden was laid with a dribble connected to his hand. Aiden was released from the medical clinic after certain hours. Matt went into his room and dozed, while Aiden was exhorted by Dr. Oliver to take dozing pills. The two of them dozed and didn't see or hear anything uncommon that evening once more.

Chapter 3:

Ridiculous Fate

Matt woke up the following day and went to wash up. While washing up, he saw that his back was covered with peculiar scratches, more like hook marks, despite the fact that they didn't have any pets with them. Aiden scoured some germ-free cream on his injury and disregarded it as crafted by a rodent, as Aiden believed that the more you feel torment, the more it will insult you. He went to the kitchen and drank some espresso. He unexpectedly recollected that he expected to awaken Aiden to help him to remember his work. He went into Aiden's room and saw that Aiden was at that point alert. 'Good day!' said Matt. 'I am so worried, I am withdrawing from my work today, I will simply go to the college in the evening. Coincidentally, I have effectively educated Mr. Lorenzo about the leave, I will rest till evening' 'alright!' answered Matt and went to do his low maintenance work. Matt was low maintenance Web designer, he wasn't proficient at it, however knew the nuts and bolts and had the option to plan diverse pages, which took in substantial income. At the point when Matt was going down the lift to go for his work, he saw an odd lady stroll into the lift, she was looking furious. 'Sai, dove vivi?' said the lady. Matt perceived that she was communicating in Italian, however he didn't have the foggiest idea how to talk it, so he turned on his portable and turned on Google Translate. He composed in Sai, dove vivi?, the importance came out to be Do you know where you reside? Matt got shocked and looked toward the lady with enlarged eyes. A noisy bell stunned him, it was of the lift arriving at the anteroom. He left, he pivoted to think back and the lady was gone, mysteriously gone in the entryway, while the lift was as yet open, as though somebody was remaining before it and the lift could detect it. Matt got a consuming inclination on his back of being watched, he rushed to his vehicle and immediately drove away to his office. At home, Aiden just woke up in the early evening. He saw that Matt was at that point gone. He murmured, and went to the kitchen for breakfast. He began cooking an egg, he went to the cooler to take an egg, when he spotted something on the table. He saw an accessory, it was dark, yet was made of unadulterated silver. Aiden grasped it and saw that a pentagram was drawn on it. He began feeling tipsy, however recaptured his equilibrium. He tossed it in the garbage bin. He shook his head and kept preparing his morning meal. He did the morning meal and began looking through the feed on his versatile. He went to the refrigerator to drink some water, when he saw that the kitchen cupboards were opened, he got stunned, he went around there to close them, when out of nowhere, the cupboards began swinging wildly. Aiden eased off, not realizing what to do, he ran into his room and shut the entryway. He was truly terrified, he remained in his space for quite a long time and at last nodded off. Matt returned home late as he had a ton of work on his hands today, so when he came, the cupboards were discovered close and he was excited when he saw that Aiden's room entryway was shut. Matt thumped on it multiple times. Aiden woke up paying attention to the thumping on his entryway, he opened it and saw Matt. Aiden said 'The cupboards were opening without anyone else when I went to the kitchen, I don't have the foggiest idea how it could happen' 'What are you saying? You could actually be seeing things. Every one of the cupboards are shut,' answered Matt. 'Goodness! Definitely, you may be correct. I have been having migraines and feeling unsteady since morning,' said Aiden, overlooking what occurred. The two of them went to their college in the evening. Aiden considered a to be's laugh as he was passing by the entryway. Chills went through his spine, he struggled paying attention to addresses and taking care of job in his college, on the grounds that occasionally he was feeling unsteady. He returned home and Matt said that he would arrive behind schedule, as he would visit his auntie coming back, who was likewise living in a similar city. Aiden was sitting in front of the TV around evening time, when Matt returned home. He carried his auntie with him 'Gracious Dear! I'm only here to see your loft'. Aiden welcomed her and gave her some espresso. After she drank espresso, she chose to return, when her eye fell on Aiden's room. 'Whose room is that?' asked her. 'It's Aiden's. Be that as it may, Why Aunt Elisa?' said Matt. 'There is somebody in there, an element! A thick element' said Aunt Elisa in dismay and ghastliness. Aiden got horrified by her words. She said farewell to Matt and disappeared. Aiden was as yet contemplative pondering his room and the element, Aunt Elisa was discussing. He was unable to rest appropriately, so he took dozing pills and he in the long run dozed. He woke up the following morning to discover a stain on his divider. He hadn't awoken as expected at this point, so he disregarded it and returned to rest as his work began at 11:00am and the present moment, it was just 9:00am. He woke up with the sound of the caution going off on his versatile, he excused the alert and woke up. He focused as an afterthought mass of his room and there it was, a similar stain, yet presently Aiden discovered that it was a stain of blood. He looked nearer and saw that with blood it was composed on the divider Your Horrific Fate has quite recently started. Aiden got up from his bed to contact the blood, regrettably, it was new red blood! He got up and hurried to Matt's room. 'There... There is a blood stain on my room's divider!' yelled Aiden. Matt scoured his eyes and strolled over to Aiden's room, however when he came to there, nothing was on the divider. Matt gave an irate look to Aiden and returned. Aiden was as yet in shock, he couldn't defend what had simply occurred with him. He reached a resolution that it may very well be his creative mind and nothing else and again the two of them disregarded it like nothing occurred. Be that as it may, they didn't have the foggiest idea what anticipated them!

Chapter 4:

Indeed! It's spooky

The following day, Matt was strolling down the foyer to go to his work . That day was a Wednesday, so Garamond college didn't mastermind any talks or practicals. To put it plainly, it was a three day weekend for their college. He again felt a shudder go through his spine, he thought back and saw a lady - a similar lady he had seen previously. She was strolling strangely, her legs were out and out shocking and she was leaving a path of dark slime any place she strolled. Matt followed her, to check whether she was a gatecrasher in the structure. She went to one side and strolled inside a dim room isolated by any remaining lofts. Matt got befuddled as he hadn't seen the room previously. He strolled gradually and marginally pushed the entryway of the room, a squeaking sound came from the corroded pivots of the entryway. Matt saw only murkiness thus quite a bit of it that he was unable to try and make out the edges of the room. He took out his cell phone and turned on the blaze light. He pointed the light in front and saw a couple of legs covered with dark seepage, however something was off the legs weren't contacting the floor, they were hanging. Matt was presently totally frightened, he was shuddering constant. He lifted up his cell phone and presently he was vis-à-vis with the draping dead body of a lady, Matt yelled truly boisterous and dropped. 'What was that?' said Axel, the Janitor of the Apartment building. He was confounded by the incredibly uproarious and uncanny yell, so he ran towards THE ROOM, since he was certain that the voice came from here. At the point when he went into the room, he turned on his electric lamp to see the room in the horrible haziness. He stepped on something while at the same time strolling, he pointed his electric lamp down and saw the virus hand of Matt. 'Wow! This... This is simply the new inhabitant' he murmured. He dialed 911 on his telephone, since he believed that Matt was dead, he even didn't try to check in case he wasn't. '911, what's your crisis?' asked the call-taker. 'The location is Brown Sea Apts. on Bettensey Road, another inhabitant who moved into this apartment complex was discovered lying (Maybe Dead) in an extra space by me, if it's not too much trouble, send a rescue vehicle at the earliest opportunity' Axel answered rapidly. 'Alright! Try not to stress Sir, we'll send help immediately' said the call-taker prior to hanging the call. Axel left Matt as he was and ran higher up to advise Aiden. Aiden was in the mean time setting up a home-task, in the wake of eating 'I'd leave for my work following 40-45 minutes' Aiden thought. Thump! Thump! He heard a thump on the entryway, he was astonished as there weren't such a large number of guests for him. He went to the entryway and peeped through the peep-opening. He saw Axel, who was gasping. He opened the entryway, and let Axel in. 'Your companion... Matt... He is discovered oblivious in the extra space. I just called 911,' said Axel. 'Pause... This can't be, Matt previously left for his work' answered confounded Aiden. 'I don't have the foggiest idea what occurred! You can come first floor and see it for yourself!' said Axel and stepped down the steps. Aiden got his wallet and vehicle keys and surged first floor. He could hear the far off alarms of Ambulances, not drawing nearer. He was stunned to see Matt, thinking in case he is even alive or not! 'The Ambulance is here!' yelled Axel and opened the Apartment's fundamental doors, the PARAMEDICS got and kept Matt's body on the cot and took him in the emergency vehicle. They took him to the clinic. Aiden sat in his vehicle and drove off behind the rescue vehicle to the emergency clinic. They arrived at the clinic quickly. Matt was taken to a crisis ward, while Aiden was sitting in the holding up region. They analyzed and treated Matt for 25 minutes and afterward, Dr. Oliver left the ward and said 'His condition isn't actually ordinary, since when he came into faculties 6 minutes prior, he hacked out some dark slime.' 'Dark seepage! In any case, How?!' asked Aiden. 'We don't have a clue, however we removed the toxin from his body, he will be all set quickly's said Dr. Oliver, 'Much obliged!' answered Aiden. He held up 5 additional minutes and afterward saw Matt leaving the ward evidently solid. 'What occurred in those days?' asked Aiden in interest. Matt checked out Aiden in dread and said 'I saw this lady... ' said Matt, yet was hindered by Aiden 'Were her legs not typical?' 'How'd you know? Indeed, they were odd. She was leaving a path of dark slime behind her' said Matt. 'That is a similar lady who torment me' said Aiden. 'I imagine that our Apartment or even the entire structure is spooky' said Matt in alarm. Both were presently alarmed. They drove back home. Matt rested in his bed and Aiden left for his work. Matt opened his PC and began composing an email to the director of his product organization.

Dear Walter,

I was unable to go to my work today because of my medical issues. I fell oblivious and must be taken to the clinic. I am sorry for any bother, however I'll ensure that I will make the site of Ms. Charlotte from home through my PC and send it to you when it's prepared. I'll go to my work from tomorrow.

Matt,

Worker of Gizmo inc.

He sent the email and shut his PC once more. Crash! 'What sound was that?' said Matt. He wore his shoes and strolled towards the kitchen. There, he saw the Dustbin had tumbled down and all the garbage was on the floor. He hit his hand on his head and took out a brush stick to tidy up. He saw something while at the same time cleaning, among the wide range of various waste was a memento with a pentagram. Indeed! This is the very memento that Aiden found and tossed in the waste. Matt got it and washed it. At the point when he wrapped tidying up, he analyzed the unusual memento. He could feel something was off with regards to it. He felt a solid cerebral pain, he was sincerely anxious. That is my memento Matt heard a murmur. He was in a ton of agony and was befuddled, so in the wake of hearing the murmur he tossed the memento back in the rubbish. His aggravation finished out of nowhere, yet he didn't realize that more aggravation was anticipating him.

Chapter 5:

The Demon

After being relieved from the headache, Matt collapsed on his bed, he took a small nap and then again opened his laptop to create a website for one of his clients. He worked for a while and then saved the project as a draft. He then closed his laptop and started thinking of the unusual events that happened with them in this house. He tried to give a rational explanation to at least one of the incidents, but failed. After sometime Aiden came back from his job, he was tired after all the smell of onions and garlic, so he took a bath again to be fresh. He jumped into the shower after a hectic day. While he was shampooing his hair, he noticed a glitchy dark figure standing in the bathroom. He couldn't see what or who it was, as to the shower curtains. He could see the figure making no movement and standing still. He was fearful thinking of who it would be. He carefully turned off the shower, changed his clothes and came out of the shower. There was... NOTHING! He was sure that he saw someone standing still in the bathroom. He quickly came out of the bathroom. He was really scared by what just happened. On the other hand, Matt was still in his room, he opened his laptop once again to complete the PROJECT, he kept doing some work for a while until he completed it. He then sent it to Walter (The manager of Gizmo inc.), Matt was now randomly checking on scrolling down his feed on YouTube and came across a video, titled: The Building of the Family Spirits: Backstory, Matt was sort interested in these type of Horror stories or Real Haunted houses, but didn't have so much time to watch videos about such haunted houses, so in hope of passing some time, Matt clicked on the video. The video showed a reportedly haunted building, the narrator was randomly talking about the history of the building 'The building is one of the most haunted buildings in its country, although the whole building is haunted, but specifically there is an apartment in this building which is the home of all the spirits, This apartment has had two families to live in it, the 1st one left soon as they had found a better place in another town or city, while the mysterious partis that no one knows what happened to the 2nd family, people say that the 2nd family dies of tragic causes, but local residents believe that the family did black magic and were corrupted by the immense control on demons, they were so ravenous for the power of evil that ended up killing themselves and now the spirits of the whole family roam not only that apartment, but the whole building, since then No tennant has shifted into that apartment for years, but the owner of that apartment claims to have rented it out to somebody. After all this, who would believe that people are still living in that building? If you still didn't get scared, then I think that the pictures of this building I am about to show you will totally freak you out' The video then displayed a series of pictures of the building, Matt looked carefully at the pictures and when the 1st picture showed up, Matt's blood ran cold! He was now looking at the picture of Brown Sea Apts.! Matt was extremely frightened, The next picture was of the elevator, which was also the same as their building. The next picture was enough to scare even his soul. Yes! The next picture was of the door of Matt's and Aiden's apartment. Matt zoomed in the picture and could clearly see the apartment number written on the door 'Apartment no. 666'. Matt freaked out! He ran to Aiden's room along with his laptop. Aiden was chatting with his Grandfather, who was living in Hamburg, Germany. When Aiden saw the look on Matt's face, he asked 'What happened?!' 'I was right! It's now confirmed' replied Matt. 'What's confirmed? I can't understand anything,' said Aiden. 'This building is haunted!' exclaimed Matt. 'What!? How are you so sure?' asked Aiden. 'This... This video. It shows our building's pictures and not only that, but also our Apartment's pictures. The narrator is saying that this building is one of the haunted buildings in the country!' explained Matt. 'Show it to me!' said Aiden. He watched the video for himself and was horrified. They were both scared. All of a sudden, the power went out. Aiden was confused, because normally there was no power outage in this area. Then, Matt saw something. 'What's that?' asked Matt while pointing to the corner of the room. Aiden looked there and saw a woman standing there, she was breathing heavily. Matt and Aiden both jumped on the bed, scared! To their horror, the woman crouched down on all her fours and walked slowly toward them. SHe was getting closer and Aiden was now getting really scared and he was about to pass out. Both of them shouted and bolted out of the room closing the room's door on their back. Then they heard some knocking on their door, Aiden was too scared to even talk, so Matt rushed towards the door to open it. When he opened the door, He saw Ms. Analise standing and behind her was Harold. When Aiden saw Ms. Analise, he ran towards her and Harold and shouted 'This house is haunted!' Ms. Analise's eyes widened, 'So, you know!' she said. Herald was sweating uncontrollably, 'I am really sorry, but I was paid a lot for renting out this apartment, so I had to. I knew that it was haunted,' exclaimed Herald. Matt got angry and said 'We are leaving this apartment right now'. 'No! It's not that easy' said Ms. Analise who felt sad for the boys. She continued 'I needed to rent out this apartment, as if this apartment didn't get rented out, it would be owned by the government under the title of A HAUNTED HOUSE, so If that happened I would've lost a lot of money, because apart from this apartment, I own other apartments in this building too and after all of them gone, I would have to suffer a lot, so I appointed Harold who was a professional Real Estate Agent, I made him sure that if he would rent this apartment out I would give him so much money' 'I don't care what you say, we're just leaving this place!' shouted Matt. 'No! You can't! The demonic power here grows every time it haunts a resident and feeds on their fear and now, it has found you as it's perfect prey. Once it's attached to you it's really hard to get rid of it!' Said Ms. Analise while crying. Matt and Aiden were really shocked, surprised and Horrified. 'Look! I believe you!, but you said that it's hard not impossible to get rid of it, so

What's the hardest way?' asked Aiden. 'Have you ever encountered a pentagram locket in this apartment?' asked Ms. Analise. '... Oh My God! Yes! I saw a pentagram locket the day before yesterday, but I threw it away,' said Aiden. 'Me too! I saw it today, but I tossed it in the trash can just like Aiden did, I also felt a headache after holding it!' said Matt. 'Yes! That's right! Give me that locket' ordered Ms. Analise. 'But, it's in the trash can!' said Matt. 'I'll get it!' Ms. Analise got up and dug into the trash can, she found the locket, she threw the trash back in the bin, washed her hands and kept the locket in Aiden's hand. 'You need to bury this locket in a far away grassland and after burying it, you need to pour salt water on that BURIAL place, then you need to come back in this apartment and chant the words Show me the light or Leave me in darkness, this way, the demon will show either one of you the light and it will leave the other one in darkness means possess the other one!' Matt and Aiden were shocked, but clearly understood what she was trying to say, she was trying to say that One will be given the chance to live and One will die!

They were waiting for what Ms. Analise would say further. But, then Aiden spoke up 'But... How's that possible? Neither of us would be ready to die! Nonsense!' 'Well! I am really really sorry! But, this is the only way,' said Ms. Analise. She had realised her mistake and was trying to apologize. 'Can't anyone else give their life?' asked Harold to Ms. Analise. 'No!' she said. 'Can't we like... just leave this apartment as simple as it is?' asked Aiden. 'It's possible, but a hard way, because if the demon finds out that you've left, it will come for you and then, it will kill any of you... The One it likes the most!' explained Ms. Analise. 'Well! We can handle an unknown death than a more known one! We'll just simply shift out of this apartment' said Matt. Ms. Analise was a little skeptical about the idea. 'As soon as you leave this place, me and Harold will give over this apartment to the government, because I can risk money, but can't take someone's death's blame upon myself!' she said. 'Good! So... we will leave this apartment today! I can stay in a cheap hotel,' said Aiden. 'And maybe I can stay at my aunt's house,' said Matt. 'Ok! But... be careful!The demon is really strong. It has fed on your fear enough to kill at least one of you!' Ms. Analise said. Matt and Aiden started packing their stuff. Ms. Analise and Harold were waiting for them to leave in the lounge. Aiden came back into the lounge and said 'Oh! Sorry!, here's your PENTAGRAM Locket!' 'Thanks! I will discard it' Ms. Analise. Harold was still regretting having to risk his life, just for a bit of money. Aiden had packed his stuff, while Matt was still packing his. It was around 4:00pm, when Matt and Aiden came to Ms. Analise and Harold in the lounge and said 'We've packed and are now leaving'. They gave the apartment keys to Ms. Analise and left. Aiden was going in a taxi and Matt was going in his car. When Aiden was leaving the building, he took a glance back at the building and he could see a dark figure standing in his (former) bedroom window. Aiden thought that that FIGURE was looking at him, but then he saw that the figure's back was on the window side, not the face. Aiden could still feel chills run down his spine thinking of what had happened to him and Matt in this house. Aiden sat in his taxi and started his journey to ***Mille Dollari Hotel***. Apart from the name, this was a cheap hotel and even gave free food. For Aiden or maybe for any living person A HAUNTED APARTMENT WITH DEMONS is worse than a cheap bad (free) service hotel. 'You look familiar' said the taxi driver. In fact, Aiden immediately recognized the voice of the taxi driver and said 'Yes! You are the same taxi driver who brought me and my friend to this building' 'Oh Yeah! My name is Noah. But... Why are you leaving this apartment?' said the taxi driver (Now: Noah). 'Because this building was very bad and the truth is that it's...' said Aiden, but was interrupted by Noah 'Cursed!' 'How'd you know?' asked Aiden in curiosity. 'That time remember! When I was leaving you both to this building I said that this building is.. And then I stopped. I was about to say that this building is cursed and haunted, because my father used to live here in his young age with his parents. They lived in Apartment no. 667, They could hear creepy noises from their neighboring apartment, APARTMENT NO. 666, so one day when my Grandpa went to investigate what was happening in that apartment, a strange humanoid creature launched at him and killed him. My dad is really old now, but he still says that the creature was a demon!' Noah explained the whole story. 'OMG! That's the same thing that happened with me and my friend Matt. Strange occurrences happened with us in the building, the only way to get rid of it was for one of us to die, so we decided to leave this building and live in different places and our apartment no. was 666!' said Aiden, which shocked Noah. 'It will kill at least one of you! Heed my warning! Stay safe. Remember! That, it can't kill you directly. It will come in a different humanoid form, probably in the shape of a person you know' Noah warned. 'But, How will I know if it's the demon or a real person?' asked Aiden. 'The only way to recognize it is that It will be very very less talkative, because If it speaks it will uncover it's deep dark voice and reality' said Noah. 'Thanks for the advice! If you would've told us all this at that time and if we would've believed you, then I and Matt wouldn't be suffering from this horror of knowing that we'll die soon' said Aiden and got really sad. They didn't talk the rest of the way. They finally reached the Hotel. Aiden was feeling like some burden of horror was lifted from over him. He entered the hotel and bought a room. He took all his luggage in the room. He first washed his face and got fresh, then he slept. From all the tension and suffering, Aiden was really exhausted. On the other hand, Matt had reached his aunt's house and was also stressed, but still he explained everything to his aunt. Aunt Elisa said 'What happened, Matt? Why did you come here with all your luggage' 'The apartment we (me and Aiden) lived in was haunted, so extremely haunted that we had to leave and you know what? The demon is still after us! And he wants one of us!' he explained to his aunt. 'That's horrific!'. 'Hopefully! You will be safe, My house is really holy, you'll be safe here' She said. Fear was engraved in the hearts of Aiden, Ms. Analise, Harold and Matt. Will one of them die? If yes! Then who will it be?

Chapter 6:

Demonic Departure

They were waiting for what Ms. Analise would say further. But, then Aiden spoke up 'But... How's that possible? Neither of us would be ready to die! Nonsense!' 'Well! I am really really sorry! But, this is the only way,' said Ms. Analise. She had realised her mistake and was trying to apologize. 'Can't anyone else give their life?' asked Harold to Ms. Analise. 'No!' she said. 'Can't we like... just leave this apartment as simple as it is?' asked Aiden. 'It's possible, but a hard way, because if the demon finds out that you've left, it will come for you and then, it will kill any of you... The One it likes the most!' explained Ms. Analise. 'Well! We can handle an unknown death than a more known one! We'll just simply shift out of this apartment' said Matt. Ms. Analise was a little skeptical about the idea. 'As soon as you leave this place, me and Harold will give over this apartment to the government, because I can risk money, but can't take someone's death's blame upon myself!' she said. 'Good! So... we will leave this apartment today! I can stay in a cheap hotel,' said Aiden. 'And maybe I can stay at my aunt's house,' said Matt. 'Ok! But... be careful!The demon is really strong. It has fed on your fear enough to kill at least one of you!' Ms. Analise said. Matt and Aiden started packing their stuff. Ms. Analise and Harold were waiting for them to leave in the lounge. Aiden came back into the lounge and said 'Oh! Sorry!, here's your PENTAGRAM Locket!' 'Thanks! I will discard it' Ms. Analise. Harold was still regretting having to risk his life, just for a bit of money. Aiden had packed his stuff, while Matt was still packing his. It was around 4:00pm, when Matt and Aiden came to Ms. Analise and Harold in the lounge and said 'We've packed and are now leaving'. They gave the apartment keys to Ms. Analise and left. Aiden was going in a taxi and Matt was going in his car. When Aiden was leaving the building, he took a glance back at the building and he could see a dark figure standing in his (former) bedroom window. Aiden thought that that FIGURE was looking at him, but then he saw that the figure's back was on the window side, not the face. Aiden could still feel chills run down his spine thinking of what had happened to him and Matt in this house. Aiden sat in his taxi and started his journey to Mille Dollari Hotel. Apart from the name, this was a cheap hotel and even gave free food. For Aiden or maybe for any living person A HAUNTED APARTMENT WITH DEMONS is worse than a cheap bad (free) service hotel. 'You look familiar' said the taxi driver. In fact, Aiden immediately recognized the voice of the taxi driver and said 'Yes! You are the same taxi driver who brought me and my friend to this building' 'Oh Yeah! My name is Noah. But... Why are you leaving this apartment?' said the taxi driver (Now: Noah). 'Because this building was very bad and the truth is that it's...' said Aiden, but was interrupted by Noah 'Cursed!' 'How'd you know?' asked Aiden in curiosity. 'That time remember! When I was leaving you both to this building I said that this building is.. And then I stopped. I was about to say that this building is cursed and haunted, because my father used to live here in his young age with his parents. They lived in Apartment no. 667, They could hear creepy noises from their neighboring apartment, APARTMENT NO. 666, so one day when my Grandpa went to investigate what was happening in that apartment, a strange humanoid creature launched at him and killed him. My dad is really old now, but he still says that the creature was a demon!' Noah explained the whole story. 'OMG! That's the same thing that happened with me and my friend Matt. Strange occurrences happened with us in the building, the only way to get rid of it was for one of us to die, so we decided to leave this building and live in different places and our apartment no. was 666!' said Aiden, which shocked Noah.

'It will kill at least one of you! Heed my warning! Stay safe. Remember! That, it can't kill you directly. It will come in a different humanoid form, probably in the shape of a person you know' Noah warned. 'But, How will I know if it's the demon or a real person?' asked Aiden. 'The only way to recognize it is that It will be very very less talkative, because If it speaks it will uncover it's deep dark voice and reality' said Noah. 'Thanks for the advice! If you would've told us all this at that time and if we would've believed you, then I and Matt wouldn't be suffering from this horror of knowing that we'll die soon' said Aiden and got really sad. They didn't talk the rest of the way. They finally reached the Hotel. Aiden was feeling like some burden of horror was lifted from over him. He entered the hotel and bought a room. He took all his luggage in the room. He first washed his face and got fresh, then he slept. From all the tension and suffering, Aiden was really exhausted. On the other hand, Matt had reached his aunt's house and was also stressed, but still he explained everything to his aunt. Aunt Elisa said 'What happened, Matt? Why did you come here with all your luggage' 'The apartment we (me and Aiden) lived in was haunted, so extremely haunted that we had to leave and you know what? The demon is still after us! And he wants one of us!' he explained to his aunt. 'That's horrific!'. 'Hopefully! You will be safe, My house is really holy, you'll be safe here' She said. Fear was engraved in the hearts of Aiden, Ms. Analise, Harold and Matt. Will one of them die? If yes! Then who will it be?

Chapter 7:

Painful Past

The next day, Aiden woke up, took a bath and got ready for his job. He decided to eat breakfast on his way from a restaurant. He was feeling really calm, although he still had the fear of meeting a demon, but he was still relieved that he was no longer in that apartment. He went down to the lobby of the hotel and called a taxi. He first went to Toothsome Morning Munch to have breakfast. He entered the restaurant, sat on a table and called the waiter. 'What would you like, Sir?' asked the waiter. 'Uh! Can you please bring a cup of coffee and a couple of French toasts, please make it quick!' replied Aiden. 'Ok! Sir' said the waiter and went into the kitchen to bring the order. 'Hey! It's you. Aren't you Aiden?' said a deep voice from behind Aiden. Aiden was all of a sudden scared, he thought that it was the voice of the demon. 'The demon won't reveal his voice' thought he. So, he looked behind and saw Mr. Earl. 'Oh! It's you. Good morning Mr. Earl' said Aiden. He was the landlord of their old apartment. 'Where are you going?' asked Mr. Earl. 'I was going for my job, so I decided to stop by and have breakfast. I don't like the breakfast of the hotel I'm staying in!' said Aiden. 'Hotel!? You were living in an apartment with your friend Matt, right?' asked Mr. Earl who was confused. 'Mmm... that apartment turned out to be haunted, so we had to leave it. Many horrific things happened to us and now, the thing we are the most scared of is that the demon is still after us. He will surely kill one of us' exclaimed Aiden expressing the fear that he had. 'That's unbelievably Sad and Terrible! I am feeling really sorry for you boys!' said Mr. Earl and left. 'Sir your coffee and French toasts are here' said the waiter. 'Oh yes! Thanks! Here you go, the money!' said Aiden. He ate his breakfast and left for his job in a taxi. 'I just would have also done breakfast in my own restaurant' thought Aiden. He reached his restaurant and worked for an hour or two and then came back to his room in the hotel. He was not too tired today, because he had completed all his sleep last night, so he opened up his laptop and searched about the history of Brown Sea Apts. He caught some articles and even found pictures of newspapers which were many years old. He found one newspaper picture riveting. He opened it up and read it carefully. It read:

A lady killed her family in Brown Sea Apts. near the newly built Garamond university, claiming that she is a demon and also threatens everyone who enters her apartment! According to police reports, she had been performing black magic in her apartment no. 666 and according to voice evidence of the woman gathered by police she has summoned a ferocious demon who feeds on fear and demands the lives of those who have lived in his resting place. Priests have done countless exorcisms on the woman, but nothing seems to work. She has even threatened other people that if they come into her apartment, she would kill herself! ---- reported by PO Carl Butter on June 30th, 1975.

Aiden was shocked by what was mentioned in the report. He couldn't believe that Ms. Analise and Harold could rent out such a haunted apartment with such a dark history. Aiden opened WhatsApp and texted to Matt 'If we would've lived a little longer in that place, this piece of information suggests that we would've been dead' and then he sent the screenshot of that newspaper, because it wasn't downloadable. Matt had just returned from his job and was washing his face, when he heard the notification sound on his mobile phone. He came out of the bathroom and checked out whose message it was. He opened Aiden's chat room and read his message, then he saw the newspaper picture. It was too unsettling for him, so he texted back 'Is all of this detail true? I can't believe it!'

Aiden replied 'I know right! It is so horrific and this news report is by Police Officer (PO) Carl Butter in 1975'. Matt read the reply of Aiden and continued 'Oh! Yeah, this is so old and after all this time, the demon would be so hungry, that he fed on our fear so much that it made it extra strong and hungry for blood'. Aiden read Matt's message and texted 'Hmmm □'. Aiden kept his mobile and started thinking of the strange and outright horror experiences that they had in this apartment. From a strange woman in sleep paralysis to a pentagram locket which gives headaches, this apartment gave them nothing but horror. Aiden was thinking of the previous events and remembered the pentagram locket. He dialed the phone number of Ms. Analise. 'Hello! Ms. Analise, I was thinking of the horrific events that happened with me in that apartment and then I suddenly remembered the locket. What did you do with the locket?' Aiden asked. 'First of all I am really sorry! I am suffering from depression by thinking that I will be responsible for someone's death. I know it's not possible for you and Matt to forgive me! On the topic of the locket, I will take it to Green Grumblers Grasslands and bury it there, then I...' She said and then stopped. 'Oh! Ok Ms Analise, I hope you bury it successfully! Thanks! Bye!' said Aiden and then he hung up the call. Ms. Analise was suffering from severe depression and Capiophobia. She was scared that she would get arrested for her mistake. Harold was also very fearful, he was continuously thinking about the loss of money he will suffer if he gets arrested by police for knowingly renting out an apartment that's haunted and dangerous for its residents. Matt was suffering from Daemonophobia and Aiden had the same problem, as he had no parents. His parents died years ago, so he lived with his uncle in a different city. His uncle was really cruel and didn't educate Aiden. One day, Aiden left his uncle's house and ran away. He reached the city center, where a man who listened to Aiden's sad origin, helped him reach the neighboring city. There, Aiden met a boy the same age as Aiden. Aiden and that boy became best friends and helped each other. They lived in an orphanage for years and were educated by a man who donated money to the orphanage. When they both grew old, they left the orphanage and lived in an apartment, which they afforded by doing a part-time job. That boy was Matt! But, now this homicidal demon broke their friendship and separated them. Aiden remembered his past and got really sad. He then went to his university. There, he met Matt, Aiden was really happy to see him. They talked a lot, after the classes, they talked for a while in the cafeteria and then went back, Aiden to his hotel and Matt to his aunt's house.

Chapter 8:

The Curse lift-off

Aiden woke up today to an odd inclination. He could feel like something just left him. He could feel like he was carrying on with a similar life he had before this loft and this frightfulness and dread. He just had an alternate inclination. He had woken up ahead of schedule, so he got up, scrubbed down and afterward checked for new messages on his portable. There were no new messages. Then, at that point, he got a call from Harold. 'That is odd, for what reason did he call me? Presently, we are at this point not connected to that condo,' Aiden thought. He got the call and could just hear the weighty and quick breathing of Harold. 'Hi! Harold, what occurred?' asked Aiden. 'Uh! Ok! Aiden!... Ms. Analise... She is DEAD! She committed suicide in the condo that you were living in' shouted Harold. Aiden quickly got stunned by the abrupt news. 'Yet, I just conversed with her yesterday!' said Aiden. 'I don't have the foggiest idea what occurred. The police are here, they are exploring the scene!' shouted out Harold. Aiden hung up the call and called Matt. Matt was conversing with his auntie, when he saw his telephone ringing, so he got the call. 'Hello! Aiden, What's up?' asked Matt in a lighthearted way. 'Matt! Ms. Analise is discovered dead in our (previous) condo!' said Aiden. 'What?!, yet... ' said Matt who was puzzled. 'I'm going to the loft! Bye!' said Aiden and hung up. Aiden quickly called a taxi and headed toward Brown Sea Apts. At the point when Aiden came to there, everything he could see were Police vehicles and everything he could hear were alarms. Aiden hurried to the entryway of the structure, there he could see a dead body canvassed in white fabric lying on a cot, which was being hauled to the emergency vehicle by Axel and the AMBULANCE PEOPLE. Aiden strolled to the dead body and could see Ms. Analise's white hair hanging out of the white cover. 'She committed suicide!' said Axel. Aiden ran into the lift and arrived at the third floor. He shot towards the entryway of Apartment no. 666. He took a gander at the door handle, which was covered with BLOOD. He entered to see Harold remaining adjacent to a puddle of blood. 'The DEMON took her blood and presently it has left this spot' said Harold. 'What!?' asked Aiden who was befuddled by what Harold said. 'Here you go! The Police discovered this note on Ms. Analise's dead body. It's for yourself and Matt' said Harold. Aiden took the paper note which was named For Matt and Aiden. He unfurled it and read:

I'm grieved! For what I did. I covered the pentagram memento in an obscure field on Green Grumbler Grasslands, I was unable to live with the weight of a Murder on my head, so I chose to commit suicide. Along these lines, I wouldn't need to fault myself for a homicide and this will likewise rest the evil presence. I forfeited my blood to satisfy the evil presence's craving. All I need presently is FORGIVENESS! - - - Ms. Analise

Aiden's eyes loaded up with tears in the wake of perusing the note. He was truly miserable, yet additionally thankful for being saved from death. Then, at that point, Matt came into the loft, he was shocked by what he recently saw. He ran toward Aiden and said 'Good gracious! This is terrible, for what reason did she commit suicide!?' 'Read this note!' said Aiden while giving it out to Matt. At the point when he read it, he additionally got very dismal. He investigated at Harold who was likewise crying not as a result of the demise of Ms. Analise, but since of the explanation that he will be captured by the police. 'We excuse you and Ms. Analise!' said Aiden to Harold. 'Much appreciated! A great deal,' said Harold got brightened up. 'I actually can hardly imagine how she forfeited herself to save us!' said Matt. Then, at that point, a truly old Police official strolled into the loft. 'Along these lines, the evil presence is resting now! Huh, young men?' said the cop. 'How would you think about the devil?' asked Aiden. 'Hahaha! I'm a Senior Police official - Carl Butter!' answered Mr. Carl. 'Goodness! You... You are Mr. Carl... the PO who announced that occurrence in 1975 with regards to the had lady, right?' asked Aiden. 'Indeed! I'm! You may be the fortunate ones to get saved!' Mr. Carl said. 'Goodness yes! Ms. Analise saved us from the ruthless evil spirit,' answered Aiden. Mr. Carl felt tragic for a brief period, then, at that point, he giggled and left. Aiden and Matt returned, Aiden was with Matt in his vehicle and the two of them were going to Aunt Elisa's home. They were too tragic to even consider talking the entire way. 'In this way, young men! What occurred?' asked Aunt Elisa. 'Our condo landowner kicked the bucket and she forfeited her life for us, presently the devil is as of now not after us' clarified Matt. 'Gracious! Express gratitude toward God! My son is protected! I realized that something was off with that loft!' said Aunt Elisa. 'Hello! Why not BOTH stay here, there is a room in the loft!, it's truly perfect and tranquil,' she proceeded. 'Gracious! Thank you kindly Aunt Elisa! You may be the best auntie Matt has, on the grounds that my uncle wasn't that acceptable to me' said Aiden. 'Well! Dear, I am not the genuine auntie of Matt, I thought that he is one day, when he was playing in the shelter, I needed to embrace him, yet he would not like to leave the halfway house, so I concluded that when he will grow up, then, at that point, I will take on him as an auntie' clarified Aunt Elisa. 'And afterward, she ended up being so decent!' said Matt embracing his auntie. Aiden was feeling desolate that he had nobody, not so much as an individual who might embrace him as an uncle or auntie, yet he disregarded it and went to the inn in a taxi to get his stuff to Aunt Elisa's home.

He was assembling the entirety of his stuff, when he discovered something in his stuff, it was an image of his a distant memory guardians, Aiden got miserable, however at that point recuperated. He returned to Aunt Elisa in the taxi. Aiden then, at that point, went to his work. He was sorry to the senior gourmet specialist for late appearance. He tackled his work, this time he was smoothly working with no strain or stress. He returned to Aunt Elisa's home (Now likewise his home). He went in there and looked at his new Attic room. He was satisfied by how clean it was! Aiden and Matt were all the while thinking about that condo, Aiden was feeling truly upset for Ms. Analise. Aiden opened his portable to look at the most recent news. He was looking down his channel on Facebook, when he discovered a video with such countless perspectives and individuals' remarks on that video were FEELING SAD. Aiden got inquisitive and tapped on the video. The video astounded him. What was the video? For what reason did it amaze Aiden? Peruse the following section to discover!

Chapter 9:

The End!

Aiden discovered a video on Facebook, he tapped on it and was astonished by what it was. The video showed an ordinary day in Green Grumblers Grassland, however at that point in the video an abrupt impact occurred on the meadow and everything was set ablaze, Aiden could see individuals going around to a great extent. Many individuals were singed in the fire. Aiden saw that the video was going LIVE. Aiden was truly sickened by the site of fire and individuals consuming in it. Then, at that point, the man making the video began yelling and his portable tumbled down and afterward the live stream finished. Aiden got truly frightened, he went on the remarks area and saw that individuals were feeling truly pitiful for it. Aiden ran down the stairs to Matt's room and showed him the video, yet Matt was additionally watching a similar video. 'Stand by... Do you recall?' asked Aiden. 'Recollect what?' answered Matt. 'Ms. Analise covered the Pentagram memento in that place!!!' yelled Aiden. Matt's blood ran cold, Aiden immediately turned on the TV and watched the news channel. From each news channel, they were just appearance clasps of the fire, then, at that point, the journalist said 'The fire-detachment has effectively stifled the blazes, yet the police are as yet looking for any consumed dead bodies or any living individual who endure'. Aiden was thankful when he heard that the blazes are taken care of now. They continued to watch the news, when after at some point, the columnist began posing a cop a few inquiries about the mishap. 'Has the police had the option to recognize the reason for the impact?' asked the journalist. 'No! Not yet, however we are as yet searching for signs' answered the PO. 'Have you tracked down any living survivors?' asked the correspondent. 'No! No survivors have been found at this point!, yet we trust that certain individuals may have endure' said the PO. 'Alright! Sir, can you additionally tell in the event that you've tracked down any dubious article in the field, which could be introduced as a sign?' the correspondent proceeded. 'Not much! We have possibly had the option to track down some significant adornments and assuming you are getting some information about dubious things, we have just discovered a PENTAGRAM LOCKET. It is in such acceptable condition, that I am amazed how it could've endure a particularly immense consuming fire!, so this memento is somewhat dubious. A few occupants of neighboring regions have announced that this memento was engaged with paranormal exercises, yet we put stock in solid evidence not free expressions of mouth!' said the Police official. At the point when Aiden heard the name of the pentagram memento, he was so stunned. 'Matt, that memento was reviled. Look! How is it possible that it would have endure!?' said Aiden. 'Indeed! What's more, I believe that the evil spirit was so furious when he discovered that it's memento was covered, it chose to copy the entire spot down!' said Matt. Aiden was truly stressed. 'Young men! Lunch is prepared, immediately come and eat, then, at that point, you additionally need to go to the college!' yelled Aunt Elisa from the kitchen. Aiden shut the TV and the two of them went to the kitchen to have lunch. 'Hello! Did you find out about the mishap impact that occurred in Green Grumblers Grassland!?' asked Aunt Elisa. 'Indeed! Auntie, it's truly awful! It torched the entire spot!' answered Matt. 'Gracious! However, my delightful hand crafted Drop bread rolls and Sausage sauce will edify your mind-set, Now please!' said Aunt Elisa. Aiden giggled and took his plate. 'Auntie this is yummier than anything I've eaten at any point ever!' said Aiden. Auntie Elisa and Matt giggled. They had the entire lunch and afterward Matt and Aiden went to their college. They were taking their last class of the day

"Physical science", when the class finished, Matt and Aiden sat in the cafeteria and talked for some time. 'Hello! I have seen that I haven't been experiencing rest loss of motion of late' said Aiden. 'Definitely! I saw it as well. That is extraordinary!' said Matt. 'Say thanks to God! This repulsiveness is over at this point. I didn't trust in these phantom things previously, yet presently, all that occurred with us constrained me to accept. I won't ever have the option to fail to remember this awful piece of my life!' said Aiden. 'No doubt! Me as well. I felt that apparitions are simply made up stories, yet presently I saw one myself!' answered Matt. The two of them drank some espresso and afterward returned home. They were in their vehicle, when Aiden said 'I felt that main houses were spooky, yet I didn't realize Apartments weren't protected as well'. They arrived at home and afterward had supper. 'How was your day today?' asked Aunt Elisa to Matt. 'It was acceptable, today was our last class of this semester, presently our tests will begin from the following week' said Matt. They had supper and afterward, Aiden went to his room in the loft. He was thinking about the revile and Ms. Analise's passing. Aiden felt so eased. Aiden concluded that he would leave his place of employment from tomorrow, since he needs to get ready for his tests.

...after 4 years...

Aiden was presently a Demolition Project chief and an Architect in a major designing organization "Falsifier". He was so effective in seeking after his profession. Then again, Matt had turned into a structural architect, and was presently living in Singapore. Aiden had a particularly bustling life. At some point, Aiden got an email from the senior Project chief of his organization. It read:

Mr. Aiden,

Being the Project chief, I've understood that the road close the popular Garamond college is excessively unfilled, so I've purchased a structure in that road. You should simply deal with the destruction of that structure and plan an exquisite Mall. The structural designers will fabricate the Mall.

Much appreciated!

Venture Manager - Mr. Lucas

Aiden was glad to be given over another venture. The following day, he went to the road close to Garamond college and arrived at the structure that he needed to destroy and overhaul. He escaped his vehicle and investigated the structure. Aiden was stunned, every one of the past occasions came running into his brain, when he understood that the structure he needed to crush was Brown Sea Apts.

The End!

www.ingramcontent.com/pod-product-compliance
Lightning Source LLC
LaVergne TN
LVHW020531160826
845677LV00015B/4001

* 9 7 9 8 7 5 5 4 5 1 9 5 6 *